DAUGHTER

a novel by Janice Lee

DAUGHTER

a novel by Janice Lee

Jaded Ibis Press
sustainable literature by digital means™
an imprint of Jaded Ibis Productions U.S.A.

Acknowledgments

Excerpts of *Daughter* have previously appeared in: *Antennae* (2009), *Joyland* (2009), *Luvina* (2009), *Action, Yes* (2010), and *sidebrow* (2010).

The author would also like to thank the following people for their support: Will Alexander, Jon Wagner, Laura Vena, Joseph Milazzo, the editors at all of the above publications, Eugene Lee, Kyung il Lee, Benny, Jeff Uyeno, and of course, Debra Di Blasi and Jaded Ibis Press.

for my mother

JANICE LEE

After Buddha was dead, his shadow was still shown for centuries in a cave – a tremendous, gruesome shadow. God is dead; but given the way of men, there may still be caves for thousands of years in which his shadow will be shown. And we – we still have to vanquish the shadow, too.

– Friedrich Nietzsche, *The Gay Science*

JANICE LEE

I wish to tell you of a vision which appeared to her in the sky,
on a night when the stars were shining and she stood in prayer
and contemplation. She saw the head of a human figure with a
terrifying face, full of wrath and threats.

I was crying out for her over and over again, and there it was, the color of splayed, a sort of bookmark half-buried in the sand: pebble, burr, grain of sand, glass. This isn't just one of those fish-out-of-water scenarios. This is a body, still, dismantling it now seems like too much and yet, I want to reach out, my head bowed in recognition slowly over the beach – though this is not a beach and this is not recognition. I'm allowed to change my mind, you know, and it's fine, really; the chest wall heaving in and out and I don't think it's dead yet, not yet, just not now, not yet. Yet. Blowing air through the pores asking what do you remember what do I remember what do I remember about you?

I can admit I was excited, as this was the proof of a competence or a space, and next to it, an emptiness in that space, like a muffin pan, the space in the air that some monster might fit into exactly, or if it is a vacuum, some tiny particles might push the body ever so slightly, causing some imbalance in this whole scene because really really there is no such thing as empty space even in a vacuum. Oh, the evidence.

There's always going to be less here then there was over there, what a creature, the extended hands, reaching for some kind of anti-matter, not to say this doesn't resemble some kind of murder scene. A silhouette in the sand, hands reaching up, hands reaching for the sky like broken rifles, a kick in the ribs. Ey?

I have unearthed the corpse of an octopus in the sand. How old is it?

The creator of the world did not fashion these things directly from himself but copied them from archetypes outside himself.

My head is full of myth.

All who came to her were filled with terror at the first glance. As to the cause of this, she herself used to say that she had seen a piercing light resembling a human face. At the sight of it, she feared that her heart would burst into little pieces. Therefore, overcome with terror, she instantly turned her face away and fell to the ground. And that was the reason why her face was not terrible to others.

Daughter, daughter, have you gone far?
Daughter, daughter, are you in the undergrowth, the sky, the stars?
Daughter, daughter, I can not find you anywhere in my memories.

JANICE LEE

This might be something, then again, it might be something else. This is only a revision of a previous image, and that is only a revision of one previous to that. Is this a giant octopus, a goddess napping in the bright desert light, or a tiny pale fetus tucked and hidden away from the threats of monsters.

The sea is a mysterious force, but there is no sea in the desert.

Where are you going? / to the land of dreams. / in a rickety bus on a rickety road.

Where is it? / far, far away. / very far.

What are you going to do there? / watch my dreams come true. / but whose dreams are these, like unripe grapes, tossed back out into the open...

In the sky, surrounding this deserted desert, a place where everything is in black and white and shades of black and white, two brothers or two god-like beings or two restless serpents in the night slither slither in the sand through the sand on the sand. They play in the sand.

They are brothers of some kind of great power, and being god-like beings, they're a smart bunch of party animals.

Jorge is the older brother. Jorge knows how to party. Jorge is a cool cool cat.

JORGE
I created a world.

JUAN
What kind of world?

JORGE
The best kind of world, the kind made by me.

JUAN
Who are the people?

JORGE
People-people.

JUAN
Are they good people? They must be good people.

JORGE
Don't worry. People are like grapes. I'll pick out the ripe ones from the rotten ones, or the ones too sour to eat.

JUAN
Like sorting paperwork?

JORGE
Like sorting paperwork.

"In order to discover your own contents
you have to investigate the inside of someone else."

JUAN
I want to help.

JORGE
You're too young to be involved in such responsible acts. But you can go get me a mojito.

JUAN
Okay.

Juan, the younger brother, sings a little note. The note wavers above his head, grows bigger, and floats over a bright, blue sea. With a loud bang, a big bang, a big big bang, the note deflates like a balloon and falls into that bright, blue sea.

Jorge holds out his hand and there appears a little miniature world, covered with sea and sand, and that sea and sand is Earth. It glows and floats up, stops midway between the two brothers. Juan looks on.

JUAN
If you pressed a stethoscope to my womb there would be the pulsating pulse of a million hungry hearts, a million tired souls, pulsating pulsating.

The pulsating pulse of a million hungry hearts, a million tired souls, continues to pulse and pulse. The pulse will not stop, only waver and diminish, but never stop. It will never, never stop.

Two serpents in the night, they slither in the night, and they only live at night. They live at night when the dreams of those tired souls reach out to them for a little bit more.

May I have some more, sir? No, boy. You can't. May I sit by your fire, please sir? There's no room here for you. May I hold your hand? No. They're filthy. But they're filthy only because they live in shit. Your shit. So why are they so dirty? Why are they so unsanitary, when it's your waste they're living in. Thank you for the shit. I've made a hut out of my shit and it keeps me quite warm. I couldn't get along without it. After all, without it I would have nothing but the clothes on my back. I'm getting used to the smell.

That unbearable smell.

The dead body is at once a body and at once a corpse. Corpses are designed to be inspected, invented, so that the inside can be instructive about the outside.

Daughter, daughter, can you hear me?

It might be someone or something after an opening up, it or she, she or me, an immediate stare through the sand. See me now. A severed individual, a severed being, a severed daughter, *are you my mother? are you my mother?*, or rather, *are you my daughter? are you my daughter?*, and it's rather hard to tell with so much sand, oh there is so much sand. Pour me over some ice, through ice, and I can only remember partial warps and lulls between night and day.

Spread out through nights there is a dark heat and a laughter or promises of a promised laughter where the laughter is aimed at an absorption of self. I am terrified of falling yet there is still only one way to work and I don't know much about this or that but I know that you, only *you*, send me to the edge darling, will I ever get out of here darling, will I fall into sand or will I spread myself through sand through nights through black and heat and the old discontents where I circle around edges, (I had told myself to use commas sparingly,,,) because when I wade through this much I can touch more than one.

I run my fingers along your belly, smooth and slick, and I feel a shiver run up my spine.

If she calls it an octopus, I call it an octopus.

Mumurs that seep into the ground, murmurs that say say say

I'm thinking,
look.
          there are white ideas and then there are
look again.
          there are black ideas and then there are
                    blurs blurs blurs
you sunned too loud

Jorge claps and a giant tornado comes and sweeps everyone away. The sand is swept away, the snake scales are swept away. Only Jorge and his brother remain. The circles under Jorge's eyes have deepened to a cigar ash and mud color that makes him look acquainted with death. He is death. Juan opens his mouth to sing, but nothing comes out.

Where did you go?

no earth
fell   upon, or
within these
[boundaries]

This is a story about an excavation. This is a story about a daughter and an octopus. But that seems obvious. This is a story about a daughter and the body of a dead octopus in the desert. The body may be that of a dead god, and the daughter intends to shed some light on the situation.

In order to discover your own contents you have to investigate the inside of someone else.

I've heard this once before.

It is true, I am too cold and starved and hateful-looking to love anyone. Taking a few crucial steps back to examine body/specimen before me, now that we've learned to take in the whole picture, exaggerating parts here and there, a ragged tear in the belly where my fingernail slipped and dug into but that's irrelevant now. An outline, silhouette of a body, the diagram of the body mapping itself out but this one has many more arms than me, falling and getting up quickly.

Am I the spectator or expert? Bent down, pulling some things out of my pocket, what will this body transform into? As I've said before, this is no ordinary octopus, there is no water. Where did it fall from? I must construct a narrative to fit this mishap, or I must fit this mishap into a preexisting one. But I am only a daughter (whose?).

Okay, reopen the case, not written yet perhaps.

Jorge is wearing a cool, black sweater. He's such a cool cat. You wish you had one just like it. Juan wears a white shirt, tattered, gray, yellow, and a perfectly circular hole under the left armpit. Jorge polishes the Earth with his shirt sleeve and smoothes out the edges.

JUAN
You know you can buy that special polishing cream at the store.

JORGE
Maybe later, I spent my allowance on this sweater.

JUAN
It's a cool sweater.

JORGE
I know. Duh. That's why I bought it.

JUAN
Right.

JORGE
I want a glass case too. To display my world in. Lend me some money.

JUAN
Okay.

Juan looks at the little people down in that dark world. Juan looks at the little people crying.

It is not enough for the primitive to see the sun rise and set; this external observation must at the same time be a psychic happening: the sun in its course must represent the fate of a god or hero who, in the last analysis, dwells nowhere except in the soul of man.

And yet the sea remains a mysterious and mystical force.

JUAN
Aren't you afraid?

JORGE
I'm not afraid. I'm not afraid of anything.
Except when it's dark I'm scared just a little. But only a little bit. And when I turn the light back on, I don't fear anymore. I'm a fearless being always fearless fearless fearless in the night.

Soldiers come and scoop up a woman from the crowd. She is scooped up in a bucket, boiled and drunk down. A raging trap. There is singing and a dress so light that any breeze could make it dance.

The dress might linger for awhile but what of the flesh? The flesh, the vanishing, the body vanishing, without a change of clothes or money or a car. This isn't devastation. It's just that winter is coming. The woman will be all right. Traces of her remain at the bar where she drank her last drink, stud.

My memory is declining, or maybe it was always that bad. People seem to have terrible memories these days. (Was I wearing a red or pink sweater Monday?) Is that by chance? I try to sort my memories, but they come in spurts and spasms, my body spurts and spasms, the octopus spurts and spasms, my memories spurt and spasm.

DAUGHTER

Someone once told me people are all like a giant sheet of glass, so that when a hurricane hits we all cry out because part of that glass has been shattered.

I assure you, if anything was not intact it has been sewn up properly, stitch stitch stitch.

JANICE LEE

A trembling compass, or trembling corpse?

This morning I'm enchanted by the grace of God, a real connection insisted on between two cluttered minds. This is a gripping thought, gripped by the mirror, restless and a center of foreseen or unforeseen circumstances. Cold and dry, thick and black, a substance softer than bone, arising from within to mix with the seawater. This isn't an analogy. I'm not sick. Only true faith lets me know these things, true faith, keeping up the good mood, looking up into the sky. I am a daughter after all. Only true faith pervades the faults of the world and sweeps the counterfeit realities away, sweep sweep. It eases my grief and gives me my strength. I am gathering my strength and am barefoot and am content.

Of the various parts of the body, there are many divisions. There are many divisions between the various bodies of the world. These divisions are related in many ways, in the various body parts of the world and various worlds. Sometimes I trail my fingers through the water. Sometimes I grab a pole, a large volume of water, and do it myself.

Various devices are used in octopus fishing:

1. The *Tauteniére* – a piece of lead with hooks attached, and a red cloth.
2. A piece of wood, with hooks attached to the top and a lead weight to the bottom. For bait, a crab or a fish is used, or even a piece of red cloth. The fisherman/daughter throws the wood out as far he/she can and then hauls it slowly back toward the boat.
3. A *supion* (little cuttlefish) mirror.
4. An octopus jar.

JANICE LEE

The sea is a mysterious force, yes, but where is it? I can't feel that ebbing, unebbing, if you turn back a little there might have been an indication, but then again, maybe not. The lesson slowly past, (but what was the lesson again?) currents of undulating blue, lines upon lines, the sand ebbs, rolls in and out, shines gold and long, a quick fight could change everything, what has the tide forced here before me?

I am a doctor, I cut things open, I examine, perform hand gestures, get the picture, sink down into adobe pits, forget, half-forget, every language has its holes. Everything can change still, and perhaps this is just another task I've been assigned to.

I wonder why I still encounter strangers when I look in the mirror.

DRAW A MONSTER.

WHY IS IT A MONSTER?

I might be a monster.

Sometimes I bleed from my ears, see a mouth open, think to spit in it. I'm right here, but today I'm not eating. I've been swimming in the sea lately. Consciously or unconsciously, there are those who are afraid of me.

[an image]

[an image]

[an image]

[an image]

EVIL-LOOKING FIN is not necessarily that of a shark (*top*). The porpoise (*second*) has a similar dorsal fin but it shows its back as it rolls in the water. The swordfish (*third*) shows its tail. The manta (*bottom*) shows two parallel wing tips.

I'm not necessarily a monster.

Sometimes I work in the garden, stick my tongue out, test the level of dust in the air. The best drinking water comes from the hose, warmed by the sun. I remember folds of skin where there shouldn't have been. I remember when I didn't have my vocal organs yet. I think I was louder before.

[image]   [image]   [image]

MIGRATING EYE of a flatfish, normal in the larval stage (*left*), begins to move, left or right according to species, as the fish grows (*center*) and winds up next to the other eye (*right*). Only one eye travels.

There are monsters.

Sometimes I can't tell which is which, so walk at a safe proximity from anything that makes a grinding sound. I am a leathery creature and can withstand surf, sun and tides when I am well-nourished. But the sun soaks through my shoes and it is dusking. Who can sleep now?

[image]

FATALLY SPEARED, a hammerhead thrashes the water in its death throes. It is a powerful fish and if hooked on a line it has been known to fight until the end of exhaustion.

[image]

CLOSE TO DEATH, the hammerhead is so weak that the hunter can approach it. The small fish are remora, which attach themselves to the shark with strong sucker discs.

JUAN
Will you shut the cellar door for me, big brother?

JORGE
I will do no such thing. The cellar door stays a cellar door and stays the way it is.

Juan had mixed feelings about his big brother. He would gripe and moan, but in the end, he always loved his big brother.

He/She pretends for a long time to be busy in the workroom.
I can barely understand you.
Sure, sure. I should have seen it coming.
Stay there with her.
It is senseless to love anything this much.

The kettle is about to boil as it rains and rains and yes, yes, I should ask her sometime, thank you sir/ m'am, or, a natural abbreviation for that abbreviated state of mind we seem to be in at times, sometimes, and I guess I do believe you, I DO believe you.

But, it is almost certain to disagree with you, sooner or later.

you can imagine hearing
frets coughing,
in the recording room
it is a performance
this imagining hearing

if you like the world, the work
if you're already imagining hearing.

I think it's really happening.

the bouncing ball
someone's watching that

a repetition
a sense of living-ness
like, uhm...
the circulation of the human body.
the gravity of a human being.

it's all EMPHASIS.

When the blackness lifts, find yourself in that tiny miniature world you call Earth. Look up, see. Juan is looking down upon you.

JUAN

I'm always driving alone walking alone. I almost clip everything, hurtled by a hundred-near disasters. I think I'm safe in my little octopus jar up here in the sky and that no harm can come to me but one day, one day the people will declare that God Is Dead and it will be me that they will be talking about not my brother because He is there and He exists but only in their hearts while I exist in their minds and minds can easily be changed.

Juan looks down and confirms in his own little heart that the dangers of the world really do exist and then he wonders what he can do.
Someone somewhere drops dead.
No one reacts.

An allegory is a paraphrase of a conscious event, whereas a symbol is the best possible expression for an unconscious content whose nature can only be guessed because it is still unknown.

(Does this qualify as an allegory?) The body becomes heavy and fragile (mine or yours?), for a moment it appears that you are moving.

The fury of violins in the background does injustice to the rhythms of our screams, strings burst forth to depict their galloping their galloping, their flying their flying, their fighting their fighting. But their fighting is not the same as our fighting. It is not the same at all.

Where do these gods come from?

The limbs of the octopus waver for seconds. Were they just ripped off and attached again? I can't recall, my vision wavers. It tasted sweaty when a tentacle reached out to touch me. We are crawling through the sand together, where are we going?

When I was little, my mother gave me two precious things. She did not tell me what they were for, but I kept them close to my heart, often speculating as to their significance. The octopus jar, I kept under my bed, for safe-keeping, but also, I thought it might help protect me from demons and other monsters that dwell in dark places. The mirror, I hung directly above my bed, so that before I fell asleep and when I awoke, I could look up onto the ceiling and see myself looking down upon me.

All voices sound different in solitude.

Sometimes the tempo of life slows down and becomes like the coagulated blood, draining from an unknown body from the sea. The sea doesn't seem to know that I'm from the sea too. Clasping my own hand I swim past rocks and coral. It is beautiful down here, and the good days seem to go by quickly, I am afraid of what I am capable of, strong sucker discs reaching out to grab me, I whisper them away, a short fit of a phantom.

This is the truth, the whole truth and nothing but the truth. This circling around in my head, this excavation, you think I've amputated my love for a god with a simple cut? You've forgotten I can regenerate an arm and the texture of my skin is of waiting and surviving, shy and solitary, I live alone. Hovering above the ocean floor, I need to eat something before I starve to death. Is this a murder scene? Grisly and a place in space of violation. (What exactly is the scene of a crime?) This is an enthusiastic octopus-handling, sobering, or a weirdly inert presence that seems to fill the space in my head with a dull, yellow glow.

This body should be handled gingerly, or important evidence will be contaminated.

But this isn't just any body, this isn't just any evidence. There's something going on here, in the stars, the darkness of your face, the air, and when God said, "Let there be light," there was light, but the brightness is slipping away.

A specter sun, a specter son, squeezes light through the space of my eyeball. What creates the monster, a blasphemy of creation, the darkness that converts the phantoms of the night into beasts, a purposeless question, the octopus that swims toward the light of the moon, marking the transition of our reality to another.

JANICE LEE

Have you ever collected anything?

No, only since I have become a character.

There is a man who throws nothing away, picking his teeth, hanging bunches of garbage above boxes along the walls. An uninterrupted procession of magazines, sharpened pencils, eggs, bright colors, telegrams, waterfalls of paper. Evidence of some kind of special effort, if only there was some kind of personal contact in the world.

There is a man who writes in a gestural duration, occupying the gaps between and under boxes, implicating them, a new way of being in the world. He writes until he is in the world, until that blackness he finds himself in becomes the page which he writes, and becomes him again.

There is a man who calls himself a painter, looks at the whiteness before him, a tiny grey figure which has already been drawn in the corner. He feels himself being propelled forward, slowly at first, then faster and faster, until he flies into the distance of some light or absurdness. Has he already drawn himself onto the once empty field? What is this blind depth that becomes flat again? He is only silent, though others in the room continue to speak.

44

There is a woman who is a composer of imaginary beings. She is on the other side, obsessed with the perimeter, retracing her steps along walls and ceilings, where she finds new sounds, echoes, whispers. They come to her when she is awake or asleep, she seeks out the voices, composes them, incorporates them into the branches of the perimeter. She walks out but is always still available as a presence. She will not be able to regain her wrists for sometime, but the door is locked now so it is safe.

There is a woman who was known to be a fact, a label attached to her foot from below, accumulated piles of transcripts under her bed. There is a note, or a space for words. There is her window, a space for air. Here, the merging of two spaces, how does it differ from a rubbish heap? All this will soon be covered with new layers of garbage.

There is a character who feels the feeling of neglect, speaks to another inside the mind, *But if I were a monster I would vomit into my hands, slurp up the entrails, eat my couch, and do it all over again. And to another inside the mind, I shall not be taken. There is redness that covers my eyes, my hands, and I only wish to transform the old world into the new. Yet, I am not a monster.* And to still another, *Am I a citizen left behind? The colored rectangles on my chest have made me a monster. But if I were a monster, I would have cat eyes, I would twist my head to be horizontal with the sun, I would send flickering lights out, make them pop inside the minds of others.*

There is a character who sits on a border, that which divides the world from that, this room from that room, this space from that one. He might be inside the walls, but that would just be silly. He collects the opinions of others, tucks them into his front pocket. He describes his life through other people, only a character on a border, inside of a border, becoming a border. Is the border the monster? Or is the dancing, buzzing fly more monstrous, an exhibition, a man digging and digging, looking for something or somewhere to rest. He washes his feet and changes his socks because he can not travel along such a narrow alleyway with dirty feet.

There is a monster who has two heads instead of one. They cannot run away from each other, even when floating arrows point them in opposite directions. They come across a two-headed snowman with eyes and mouths, but there is something missing. What would make the snowman less monstrous? To affix two noses? To have one less head? Is the monster more monstrous than the snowman? How deep is the ocean of questions that separates four heads, cold to the touch, smelling and seeing and tasting.

There is a monster who knows how to read a map, who has a mother, who cares about safety, who loves bubbles, who has an imagination, who has no manners but maintains cleanliness and a state of good oral hygiene, who wears boxes for shoes. There is no one around, but what is always carried with the monster in his arms? He can play two different melodies, one fast, one slow, on the same instrument. This is called cooperation. Do monsters cooperate differently? There is standing in a puddle of something, a puddle is gathering on the other side, bubbles are floating and there are many, many boxes. The boxes are empty, except for the two walking away, filled with furry feet.

Do you have a mother?

It's quite probable, but I'm not the one to ask.

There is a monster who speaks in gibberish, the gibberish is not gibberish, but does not sound like ours. He likes to share, sandwiches and jazz music, but shapes are a little bit harder to grasp in this light. It is a bright, sunny day.

Do you remember your mother or father?

I don't remember their faces.

No, only since you eve a character collecter.

Have you eve you eve I haracted a characted anythince you eve I have becollecome become I have I haracter chave become I haver.

Have you ever character characted anything? No, only since anything? No, only sing? No, only sing? No, only sing? No, only sing? No, only sing? No, only sing? No, only sing? No, only sing? No, only sing? No, only since anythince a come anything? No, only since a chave a collecome becter come anythince anythince

There walls of personal effort, if only throws nothing away, pickind of paper. An uninterfalls. Evidence of some kind of man who the waterfalls. Evidence of some kind of papersonal effort, if only throws nothing his telegrams, eggs, bright colors, bright contact in the waterrupted procession of man who there is telegrams, sharpened pened procession of man who the waterrupted procession of pened procession of man who the waterrupted procession of personal effort, if only the world. There is along

The fin. He inder becomes the who world. The ing thation, a nestural dural he writess the world. The writess them, untion, and untion, is is ing there fin a mand until the who world. He fin world. The fin again a new world, a ges ander becomess untin the finds himplicat between the writes there page gain blacknesturatil the writestural the pagaing is and boxes hicat becomes himplich he gain them, until durat between between world. He whimplich himself becomes, of becomes a mandere gaps bein a

He is a man who calls himself onto the room continue to speak. There is a man who calls himself being propelled forward, slowly at first, then faster and faster and faster and faster, until he flies into the distance of some light or absurdness. Has he already drawn in the corner. He is only silent, though others in the corner. He feels himself onto the distance of some light or absurdness. Has he already been drawn in the distance of some light or absurdness. Has he already been drawn himself a

She perimeter, regain her steps a woman wher someter. Ther of imaginary be able able to ther who it is steps a come to regain her wrists for is on the door is a presence. She perimeter. She is a presence. They cometer, regain her side, but the door as along walls a woman who it is along her side, but being her of ther side, but them, incorporates ther steps a presence. Ther of the is and ceilings. She door so is still available to regain here is on the will available to regain her side, but the

Ther here is a space foot from be a space for window, accumulated will soon bed. Ther window, a woman who was known to heap? All soon bel attached to bed. Here is will soon be a rubbish her window, a space foot from be a space foot from be a words. Here, this heap? All soon be covere is a label attached window, accumulated to below, a spaces, how does it differ be a fact, a fact, a rubbish heap? All this a spaces, how does of transcripts under bed. Thered window, a layers of transcripts under

Ands rednes, eyestill a cat itheade cat mind, end ther a mitill ould to anglester ing of negleft cit be slurp ing les, I wout eat hand vominside againg of I a mind thester it if I would there send, ands overed to my hat behin. Ther I speat be not harails, slurp to flinto a could ther. The theaks the entall wout is to be therednes thers thanot ind sh to to speade to me ands, eyes, sen monside colorm I worm pop ther I sterect, slurp inst behinst a chem I wout, I ang lights re againglect, monside my

He collects the border the world from that room from that which divides them into his life through other people, only a character who sits on a border the monstrous, an exhibition, a man digging a border the opinions of other people, only a character who sits on a border, inside of a border, that which divides them into his front pocket. He describes his socks because he can not travel along such a narrow alleyway with dirty feet. There is a character who sits on a border, inside of a border, inside

To affix two noses? To affix two noses? To have one less monster who has two noses? To have one less heads, cold to the touch, smelling and tasting. What would make the ocean of questions. They come across a two-headed snowman with eyes and seeing arrows point them in opposite directions. They come across a two-headed snowman? How deep is the snowman? How deep is the snowman less monster more monster who has two noses? To have one less monstrous than the monster who has two noses? To have on

Do monster who has an imagination. Do monsters boxes for shoes. There is burning in his is burning away, filled cooperation, who knows how to read a map, who wears boxes are floating away, filled cooperate different melodies, on the two differently? There is a map, who has and ther, who wears but maintains cleanliness and the two walking away, filled with furry feet. The boxes for the same instrument. There is no one fast, one slow, one fast, one are many, manners but maintains cleanliness an ima

Do ask.

Do you have probable, but the one to you have probable, but to ask.

It's quite one one one to you have the a mot I'm nothe one a mot I'm not ther?

Do you have one probable, but to ask.

Do you have probable, but to you have probable, but to ask.

It's quite one probable, but to you have a mothe one a mot I'm nother?

Do a mot ther?

It's quite one probable, but I'm nother?

There is not gibberish is a monster who speaks in gibberish, the gibberish is a bright, sunny day. There is a bright. It is a monster who speaks in this light, sunny day. There is not sound likes to share, sandwiches and jazz music, but does not gibberish, but does not sound likes to grasp in gibberish is not sound like ours. He like ours. He likes to grasp in gibberish, the gibberish, but does not sound likes to shapes are a little bit harder to shapes and jazz music, but does not sound likes to

Do your or or father or father their or fatheir your their ther faces.

I don't rember faces.

I don't remember?

I don't rember mother?

I don't rember or motheir mother you rememember faces.

I don't rember ther father?

Do you remember father ther or father father ther?

Do your faces.

I don't remember or or you rememember faces.

Do you rememememember ther ther you rember or or or or mother?

I don't rememememember your mother mother their mother?

Do you remember your mother?

Do you rember

No, thank you.

There is a daughter who is an excavator of dead gods, slapping down a stone path, with a stick in one hand, a mirror in the other, a gatherer of worries and prayers, a jar full of whispers and echoes. She leaves the lights on late, often wonders what just happened, the lights still on in the morning, and she already miles away. Does she hesitate because she sees her memories in the scars, or to catch a glimpse of her tears, one by one, a reflection meant for no one but her.

There is a god who was said to be the savior of all people, the giver of nourishment, the spreader of peace. There is a god who evades deductive reasoning, absorbs your sins and grows them outwards, thick skin of blisters, sores, trailing salt and puss. He is sweaty from the work and so sometimes is two and not one. A two-headed god is twice as efficient, twice as horrifying, twice as loyal to his people. Every possibility is welcome.

Shy, to the bone, picking up the erased pages and I am rasped upon. The tentacles flap straight to my ears, my eyes work in reverse, and here is the sweetness I lick off my fingers and dip into again, dip, rip, somewhere in the world, a person wields a symbol. Here is the symbol, mouth open, come home, I don't need to understand why, but I do need to touch slick, downstream, body. Shall I grieve a bit?

Only a body, your body, a body of a monster, old wounds spilling out of sand, spilling out of eye sockets, how disappointing when the tide doesn't come back in. Do we have a case here? Where do I start? Scalpel?

And really, I feel like this is an intrusion, grand slam floored and desire. I doubt that digging is really this easy. A wail from ahead indicates a so-called mother complex.

My mother was going to die. When she didn't, I was disappointed.

God is not a permanent construction, but I lie in bed pretending to be a child, waiting for a direction in which I should move, shake, and determine the history of this moment, right now, but all I can think about is my mother who waits outside for a brave girl to emerge from the dark room, and the darkness envelops me and I gaze up and gaze down, and it is only me gazing down at myself, not God, and I am thirsty but dare not shout for water, dare not sit up, dare not undo the ties around my ankles, I feel like rolling in the mud, a rolling distortion of being, I am not a monster but when I look into the mirror it is not me who looks back at me, in my head I am rolling down a hill but there is no mud, empathy eludes me and it seems I've just struck a discontinuity of consciousness, I'm growing up rapidly and repeatedly, and each time it happens my mother waits outside to check my progress, nodding and wincing, she loves her daughter but does not want to let her go, she loves her daughter but is afraid of her, yield to the mother who kneels before her daughter, the daughter who yields to no one, whose memory is fading and the memory of a mother once is of long ago, and only a black dress eludes her sight, a replica of a memory, today she can only remember a red cloth waving in the moonlight, a familiar face, a division of parts, an ancient excavation, the eyes.

We must surely go the way of the waters, which always tend downward,
if we would raise up the treasure, the precious heritage of the father.

True, whoever looks into the mirror of the water will see the whole of their face, but the mirror does not flatter, the mirror lies behind the mask, and yet, there is no water here, and I cannot see my own horrible face, I mean, what a happy thing.

HUMAN

Pardon?

JUAN

I'm always driving alone walking alone.

HUMAN

Pardon?

JUAN

I can no longer flash a light inside a character, paint a figure like those figures with a momentary language, but I know that the greater truths reside in the necessary fiction or nonfiction that span human and more human and even human and time.

HUMAN

But who are you really? Are you my Mother my Father my Lord?

JUAN

I am many people at once. I am a mother a father a dictator a servant a brother a serpent and the most agile actor His world has ever known.

HUMAN

Do I know you?

JUAN

You may know me. You do know me. But you don't know me. I am an amiable creator who lacks enough experience in creating. I like to think I can be personable and whatever I possess is more or less the result of a talent I have for making you feel good about yourself when you are with me in the night. I'm not a seducer but I can seduce you in the night when you pray and are insecure and at your worst.

HUMAN

When?

JUAN

In the night always always in the night.

HUMAN

Why can't I hear you?

JUAN

I am hardly heard. I won't speak untruths to you but perhaps you may mishear me after all I speak loudly but you are deaf and your hearing is not too good because you are only human. I won't pass any easy compliments or odious offerings of flattery and I don't ask for them but when I do it is always in the night. We created. Both of us together. And I make do with onhand materials, what I can chip out of you, your natural ore. And then, and then, I fuel the fire of your most secret vanity.

JANICE LEE

It is the world full of water, where all life floats in suspension; where the realm of the sympathetic system, the soul of everything living, begins; where I am individually this and that; where I experience the other in myself and the other-than-myself experiences me.

A meeting with a shadow, where fishes or dwellers of the deep look up at me out of the bright blue, harmless, but it draws me near and it is haunted. A current of departing water, blue, packing sand on the ground and someone finally decided to give it a try. Do you have a name? So, I am afraid, a bit timid perhaps. I admit the insincerity in this encounter, but you are not much of an encounter, just a steady rip in my consciousness to get to the bottom of things, or the ocean, and I'm not sure where the ocean is from here.

Head, plunged into sand, this is what empathy is. Embrace and suckling, this is what sympathy is. Who are you, a thump in my coop, I search for, pine for, a putting-back. I can now envision a door.

JORGE

Who am I? No one has heard me. No one has seen me. I live on my own credit. Am I even alive?

JUAN

Of course you are. If I'm alive, then you're alive. And if you're alive then you are alive.

JORGE

You think that you're good and that I'm bad. But that's not how it is. I create and end. And you create and end. We're the same.

JUAN

We're not the same.

Living to appease myself and it's *that* that I'm drowning in. Blue, green, who knew I could be so gentle, waves streaming down my cheeks, has the tide come in yet? I was such a such a such a– or I am such a such a such a

And then I don't know how to call, how to label such mediocrity, a set of diaries beating beating through my fingers and then a cat comes, the unsuspecting mousey is naive. Look at it won't you? Who knew I would come back to myself? Waves streaming down buildings, knocking over walls and people, flood of blue and green, look at me I said. I'm beating. I'm here. I'm going forward, backward. Over and over again. Waves streaming. Look at it. (Falling a graceful fall.)

JANICE LEE

Legend has it that many creatures of the sea often perch themselves upon the crests of waves to gaze up at the moon, sitting in that space where the clouds enter the world from the bright spot in the sky, pouring out sentimentalities and absorbing the latent energy of the sun. Legend has it that an octopus, so enamored with the light of the moon and so obsessed with its brightness, will swim toward the moonlight reflected by the ocean and run aground. Perhaps it is only legend, but I recall a dream when I lit a fire on the beach to keep myself warm, and awhile later saw a familiar face swimming towards me. Though, it was at that moment I awoke to feel the sunlight warming my cheeks and my own face gazing down at me.

The distance which has allowed me to become spectator, the body to become specimen, the specimen to become me.

I drift from one self into another, clasping tentacular detail, mouth held into night, a liquid hand drifting. The carcass trembles and floats, *qualis spectator pereo.* A fusing, a brownish tint, and the shadow is fishing for octopus. Blanched and without intention, the body is quiet, our bodies are quiet, becoming the desert and encircled by hugging hands, points with fervor, swallowing the breaths of the sea.

Our planet has the wrong name and in truth we come from the sea, dismantling ages and yet, there was no sea.

THE OCTOPUS EYE (*right*) is physically [an image]
like the human eye, and is part of the most
highly evolved nervous system found in lower
animals. Similarity of eyes does not indicate
that man and octopus are closely related, but
rather means that each developed the organ
independently. This phenomenon is called
convergent evolution.

♪ Under the sea...

Like a relief map, pocked and streaked, it is always dusk out here, and dusk will always be dusk falling like thoughts onto my bed, like an abyss, no light reaching into the realms of a hidden consciousness.

I may have the bends, having descended to significant depths, the nitrogen forced into solution, pressure falling, rising to the surface, the nitrogen turning back into bubbles of gas and now allowed to dissolve, obstructing my blood vessels, cramping my joints, I think– I think–

Are we talking about the octopus or me? Once in awhile, a dead octopus washes ashore, tossed onto the beach by waves. But as I've mentioned before, there are no waves here, where are we again? Am I becoming a blur or are you? Keep me on the edge over the edge under the edge at the edge–

The long arms attached to a fleshy blob, the arms curl around my neck. But I just imagined that. I've imagined a lot of things.

JANICE LEE

Really, we are all just ones living in a world full of ones wanting to be more than ones.

JUAN
I want to be more than a one.

JORGE
Shut up, Shut up.

The sand retains few scars to remind us of its instability. There seems to be a lot of white noise coming from along the skyline, but not static, perhaps the desire for an ocean view, head turns to look left, then another head turns.

[foghorn]

quiet. really, really quiet.
like those rabbits that parody former freedom.
a sea wall
assisted by the covering.
one for a time
then two,
then two.

[foghorn]

a torrent of debris, pieces of the earth from every continent on a watery journey, winnowed and ground, assembled and reshaped, armies of sand on the march.

quiet. really, really quiet.
around the edges
flat flat rough
swimming flat, tracing lines on red murals.
curl into oneself.
what is it about the eye?
why doesn't the eye work when it rains?
and it's raining all the time...

JANICE LEE

Sometimes, the cluster of arms, it talks to me. Like an esper it peeps my thoughts, I look into the mirror, and see only myself.

She stood on a mountain slope with a deep valley below, and in it a dark body of water. She knew in the dream that something had always prevented her from approaching the lake. This time she resolved to go to the water. As she approached the shore, everything grew dark and uncanny, and a gust of wind suddenly rushed over the face of the water. She was seized by a panic fear.

The dreamer descends into his own depths... Man's descent to the water is needed in order to evoke the miracle of its coming to life. But the breath of the spirit rushing over the dark water is uncanny, like everything whose cause we do not know–since it is not ourselves.

70

Drums, dual drums that beat on my heart. I can hear the nothing. Botherrrrrr, keep moving keep moving, dark things that slither in the warm recesses of my brain, come again? A map, a map, I just want to be okay with fear. What is that shiny object? I want to hear something that makes a difference to me. I am not comfortable calling anyone my friend. I wish I could play the harmonica so I could make music when I open my mouth. Scars are keepsakes – poof –

The divisions of the brain, the soul heavy like lead, the knot or knot or knot, the octopus or "devilfish" or god or body or arm.

It seems like a creature designed for flight, and yet I pursue. It is by looking that the octopus understands.

Touching the body, the closeness of our bodies enthralls me. I would gaze on the Host, soft-eyed like pulpy mantle or disconnected eyeball looking into the eyes of my beloved.

You are almost a truth
a SCIENTIFIC truth
a SCIENTIFIC monster.

*Mankind has never lacked powerful images to lend magical aid
against all the uncanny things that live in the depths of the psyche.*

I am a God-fearing creature, or a God-loving one, whichever more aptly describes my current situation.

I am a daughter, a child of God, and if I squint hard enough, I can see the benthos, the bottom of the sea.

This desert, like the abyssal plains of the sea, is far from the monotonous expanse you might imagine. There is a slope of no more than one part in one thousand – completely beyond the ability of the human eye to recognize as anything but perfectly flat. They are usually composed of slits and silts that have accumulated over millions of years, filling in and leveling the previously irregular topography.

JANICE LEE

A girl below closes her eyes and dreams.

Above, JUAN closes his eyes and dreams.

JUAN dreams of meadows and daisies, lemonade and sandwiches. He dreams of flying and he dreams of peace on earth. He dreams he is as cool as his brother.

It took more than a thousand years of certain differentiation to make it clear that the good is not always the beautiful and the beautiful not necessarily good.

And yet, *omne superius sicut inferius.*†

---

†As it is above, so it is below.

Are you my mother?

I'm not myself these days. My interest wanes with the withdrawal of texture. There is not enough interior space in the body, and yet the distance allows a different kind of spectatorship. Is this the end of my exploring? Will I arrive where I started? Am I knowing this place for the first time? There is a fear of personal extinction and synchronicity. I am touching the octopus's heart, or is it touching mine?

Somewhere or other, overtly or covertly, I seem to realize that I've always been possessed by a supraordinate idea, that as I gaze deeper and deeper into this body, realize that this is a god, or a god being created from the outside, as dying is a step closer to a real analysis of a corpse. Is this a god-man image, or vice versa? If every cause has a cause and behavior repeats itself, probing and probing, the probe probed and groped, what is developed in these different generations? What contradictions incarnate might lie in the sun, the moon, the stars, all of which lie inside you too. What does it matter, if after all Jesus was a rabbi, if the octopus can only remember for a few days, and has already forgotten its own creation.

JUAN

I am capable of suffering and suffer now.

JORGE

I will teach you the science of God.

JUAN

Shut up, shut up!

God is buried, like a honeycomb within her brain.

The anticipation engulfs me, a gradual reddening of senses, an involuntary transformation into another living form, growing into a great light. I am redeemed and redeemer. The moon glides into the sea. There is an attempt at being. I dissolve and am an orphan. I cry for help.

JANICE LEE

AUTOPSY   1. Seeing with one's own eyes, eye-witnessing; personal observation or inspection.   2. Inspection of a dead body, so as to ascertain by actual inspection its internal structure, and *esp.* to find out the cause or sear of disease; postmortem examination.

OED.

God must be a bear, arms outstretched, ready to hug and feed you honey, my child, and it is sweet.

Nosce te ipsum, and yet it is impossible to know our own bodies in that way. Often, like a disease, the uterus operates according to its own laws, traveling at its own pace, yet demonstrated by a token presence: blood. Still, fit to fall, and it seems that what someone has brought us is the body of a dead god. The daughter cries out, "I never looked like that!" Of course recalling that we have been made in God's image, but where do such morphological calibrations exist? Where is such an authentic body that an image becomes an image or a repertoire of images that is the body? So the reservoir of a voiceless voice, an orphaned daughter or an orphaned void:

> *Only through shaking off this burdensome body could the soul achieve union with God.*

Is that not what we are looking for?

In these remains of a dead god who once was great, will my right hand be permitted to push into the swellings of such a perforated narrative? Slowly but surely, I am sure that I hear those bodies speak to me, and I am inclined to hear and obey, but as my fingers rub against the contours, it is the finitude of this world, this body, this slime, that strikes me. Which voices must I follow in such an inspection of a dead king, will I discover the tickings, tockings, defects, anatomizing what cannot be anatomized. A slight pause.

Father/Mother, I have a mind to be acquainted with your insides.

It is now. I begin. Scalpel, please.

Not a drop of sweat trickles down my breasts or sides, and as if a dream I feel a smooth-edged razor tenderly slicing in, the heart pitter-patter (is that my heart or the octopus'?) and my bare hands, becoming mottled, dark brown, enjoying the sensation of grazing against the bare flesh.

And so the daughter is orphaned again, and the daughter is not a void but a gap between spaces – spaces that correspond to claps of thunders, of melodies, of holy teeth grinding, clapping. She is not orphaned for she has her Father who art in heaven but he does not hear her for he has orphaned many – voices of tongued creatures like claps.

So does she follow? Or as an orphan does she wander within herself, her body emblazoned and orphaned and wandering and what has she become? She cuts into a flesh that is not hers but of the octopus, into a flesh that is of the octopus but also of her, and yet it is not her own flesh that she cuts into. But if it is not hers, why does she cry out in pain?

Surrounded by hourglass sand and at the edge of an introduction, the only tools needed are the knife, the mirror.

[mirror]:
          as a doubling, as doubt, as those supporting
          branches which I cling onto, and in it I see
          the drawing of breath from rays, raising
          up and walking towards those heights,
          a tube connecting me to my Father,
          and yet somewhere or another, one is
          always possessed by a supraordinate idea,
          dissolving the projections or projecting
          those lost memories outside of myself.

          after all, the world, a primitive one at that, is
          more or less a fluid phenomenon within the
          stream of my own fantasy, where subject and
          object are undifferentiated and in a state of
          mutual interpenetration.

          a story of the daughter and the octopus.

          shall we dance?

[knife]: aka the scalpel, the one that helps to find
aliquem alium internum, a certain other
one within (what do your insides look
like?) and we are confronted with the
metamorphosis of the gods at every
new state, the prophet rises up in the
unlikeliest of places, and anyway the loss
of the past becomes insignificant for the
saviour is lost too, and the savior is that
insignificant thing or else arises out of it,
a daughter, a stone, a furrow, so that the
daughter/child is both beginning and
end, an initial and terminal creature,
the flesh to be cut open and bled out, or
swept away by the sea.

It was insistent, the corpse, in the daughter's careful execution of the process, as if the octopus was asserting its physical presence all the more that she cut into it.

Doctor, exactly how many autopsies have you performed in your professional career?

I can only attest to my activities on certain days, communications with the dead often arise in memory gaps, and rather than involve myself in some ridiculous pursuit, I'd prefer to just say I'm usually making my way to church in the morning.

When did you first observe the body in question?

I'm not sure I can admit such things without contradicting myself. The environment around here, it seems to be withering. Can you feel a certain deadness in the air?

What condition was the body in when you first saw it, Doctor/Daughter?

I was in a state of hysteria. No, I was looking in the mirror, to better understand myself, to, at that moment of discovery, look into and understand my soul. I was furnished with words, so many words. There was a slight gurgling in my belly. I wanted to reach out a limb, but felt like a sinking ship, sinking back into the sand to take the place of the body. I paused and paused again. I could not find the subclavian artery, as if it had been ripped out, and for a moment, could not sense my own heartbeat. I muttered to myself, the objects of my mind like secrets floating on waves. I had thoughts, like a poet, mingling and habits imitating. I repeated and repeated myself, with replies only, something mean and menacing about the corpse in the sand. I was far from heaven, faith scarcer than the dark, a practicality keen on having nothing to do with life, perhaps, a mistake. I felt ambiguous, amorphous, needing clarification, needing clarification now. A dream of the open sea. A dream of silver water and tumbling walls. A dream of a good god, a shameless god, an exposure like floating in a hot air balloon. I may be confused, a flattening of my body areas, an absence of any reflex in the eyes when the light shone in them, a pronouncement of death, from above.

What exactly did the autopsy reveal, Doctor?

That two brothers stamp their feet before climbing the steps. That they stand in awe of numbers, but the octopus, at arm's length, turns soft and drops. That squirts of holy water exiting from the funnel act like geometrical diagrams or maps, an hourglass full of sand, a traveler finding her way home. A daughter growing inside a belly, swelling like apple blossoms, the octopus is a good observer. A female, building a wall of stones to seal the entrance to her cave, strings of unhatched eggs hanging from the ceiling, squirting holy water to keep the eggs clean, what is the color of a fading language?

Daughter, is there more?

I peered into the body, the mantle, and saw my own hands reaching back at me. I peered into your eye and realized all this eye had seen is mine and more. I shuddered. This is all projected in the form of mystery or legend or a pair of friends and the deeds we perform, we or she or you or I, the sphere of consciousness, or perhaps, this all need not be documented here.

JANICE LEE

The *"child" is therefore* renatus in novam infantiam. *It is thus both beginning and end, an initial and a terminal creature. The initial creature existed before man was, and the terminal creature will be when man is not.*
(swept away by the sea)
(under the sea)
(floating in the sea)
(drowning in the sea)

One of these days, we will all fall from God's grace, his empty, suffocating, embrace.

Daughter: If I translated this feat into sine waves, would that experience translate over into your head? Or we can invert the process and switch the peaks. Would you feel it accurately then, would you feel that inversion in your gut, that rolling back in your eyelids as I flounder around on deck gazing up at you?

Reply: Are you my mother?

The octopus is an unconscious mind.
The daughter, fully conscious, remains in a projected state, inaccessible.
By descending into the unconscious, the daughter puts herself in a
perilous position, for she is apparently extinguishing herself.

There is another texture of waiting, rougher than skin, dissolving corporeally into my own rough little being. I am probably not symmetrical, but know what not to eat in such a dissociated state.
JUAN + JORGE

We were always there, only you did not notice us.

I heard someone say once, "I am but a sock-puppet on the hand of God," but if my hand is inside you, where is yours? *Summum bonum*, I peer into the red, holding this knowledge in silence, in common, this is the first time I've written this sentence, sentence. What kind of monster are you, a dead one, a dead god, and yet gods die all the time because they do not mean anything, being made by human hands and with my human hands, I cut. A certain other one, within, these abyssal plains, the irregular topography of your skin, I cut. A body, trainable, mottled-brown, like flensing the insulation off a whale, I cut. I cut, once in awhile, a dead octopus will wash ashore, tossed onto the beach by waves, oozing fugitives of the sea, but here is a desert. *You are supple as leather, tough as steel, cold as night.*

Man woke up in a world he did not understand, and that is why he tries to interpret it.

Facts:
- An octopus has been unearthed by excavation.
- I am a skilled dissectionist.
- The octopus, like flotsam and jetsam, belong to the finder.
- It is possible to experience cutting and being cut open at the same time.
- I am supple as leather, tough as steel, cold as night.

Were you able to form an opinion as to what caused these injuries?

[image]

THE MIMIC OCTOPUS (*left*) is the most extreme example of mimicry, or protective coloration, or both (or something completely different). It can assume the shape and coloration of almost any animal it sees (*below*). It has been seen in the shape of a jellyfish, with its arms flared out and the tips tucked under; a sea snake, where all but two of its arms are balled up, and the visible ones stretched out and striped like a snake; a mantis shrimp, where the octopus lies buried in the sand, exposing only a couple of arms, which it makes look like the shrimp; a flounder, where it stretches all eight arms behind it, flattens out on bottom, and adopts the coloration of a flatfish; a stingray; and several others. The "reason" for this unusual behavior is unknown, and the species has not yet been named.

[image]   [image]   [image]   [image]   [image]

My younger self as my mother, turns back her face, suffocates in the water, the body quiet.

Inside the body lives water, speaking, water, sinking in the sand, water, only God sees the absence of metaphor. I will probably die soon but am not afraid.

It is easier to repair a broken pump than it is to heal a broken metaphor, especially when we have forgotten the difference.

By descending into the unconscious (octopus), the conscious mind (daughter) puts itself in a perilous position, for it is apparently extinguishing itself.

Yet, where is God in all this?

Carcasse, tu trembles?
Tu tremblerais bien davantage, si
tu savais, oú je te méne.

Once, on a hike by the ocean, my mother told me: don't drink the water, or you will sicken and dissolve in it.

But the seawater doesn't know I'm seawater too.

This is a wild renewal, and yes Father is coming, after the end of all things, the form in the air will have breath, this body gathered here, your mind before me, moving, the quivering of breaths, *forms, forms, and renewal*, is this an enactment, a shadow after the form, a sieve full of water, raining onto the driest sand, words that come by *mouth or letter*, this is a self-intending discovery. There's nothing strange about this encounter. It happens all the time, is happening right now. Surely you have heard this all before.

The world may seem more or less a fluid phenomenon within the stream of our own fantasy, where subject and object are undifferentiated and in a state of mutual interpenetration, yet like the legendary Hy-Brasil, bisected like two halves of a walnut, an illusory state placed on a map and copied without regret, carrying on a tradition, the hegemony of the eye. I cut off a small piece of the body, feel a tiny tingle run up my arm, out through my elbow, they say reentry is a critical and dangerous moment, and anatomy, which literally means dismemberment, would rest upon a disruption of the body's ongoing relations with the world, the sand blowing into my face, and you will probably die soon but don't be afraid, as these fragments are all a picture becoming clear. I eat the octopus meat, thick and chewy, a part of a consecrated body, sharing in the substance of God, yet the one primarily in need of redemption here is not the daughter, but the god, lost and sleeping in matter. Have I swallowed a piece of God here? I congeal, a quick lapse of memory, this depersonalization reported as "soul traveling," experimenting a simple epileptic aura and I can hear the distant sound of heavenly choirs. A sneeze, a footstep, an echo. And she thinks she hears the voice of God, "You will be healed, your tears have been seen." But it was not I who was cut open, but the octopus, stagnating, still, a lone, long, drawn-out breath.

JORGE

It needs more water.

JUAN

Does it? I think there might be too much water.

JORGE

Silly brother. It is the ocean that serves as both the womb and tomb, the cradle of mankind.

JUAN

I guess I'm a fan of things that have dual purposes.

JORGE

Yes, it's called efficiency.

JUAN

Jorge?

JORGE

Yeah?

JUAN

Do you ever get lonely up here?

JORGE

I've got you.

JUAN

I know, but, the people down there, they've got so many neighbors to depend on.

JORGE

Yeah, but they're not satisfied with any of that. They're still always calling on their Father who art in heaven, and even when we don't answer, they insist on filling in the blanks.

JUAN

Why don't we answer?

JORGE

We don't need to. They've got everything they need down there, inside themselves.

JUAN

I don't get it.

JORGE

You will when you're older.

JUAN

Oh, okay.

Our task is not, therefore, to deny the archetype, but to dissolve the projections, in order to restore their contents to the individual who has involuntarily lost them by projecting them outside himself.

My neighbor is a real charmer, a cause for wonder, a buoy in the wrong place at the wrong time, or maybe not, though it is a question of who has set it at that particular point. This is no disguise, but as we proceed with such conversations, my face begins to smooth, the twigs in my throat break into tiny digestible pieces, awaken with a rhetorical glance into the mirror.

Self-dissection is here an act of confession, and I feel I have so much to confess, *Father forgive me for I have sinned,* but my Father who art in heaven does not look down upon me, watch over me, drip honey down my ragged throat, it is only a reflection of a transitional face, pockmarked and ragged, I only hear a soft "no" murmuring, I feel as if I'm in a body not my own, and this constant sense of deja vu, I've been here once before.

This is a story of a daughter who is that hermit who seeks the desert's solitude and emptiness to confront the ultimate reality of God.

Our minds already extend out into the environment, and the changes we make to the environment already alter our minds.

An abortive birth is this:

> She holds a mirror and knife, yet this is not
> a Medusa myth. She wields the knife as a
> scalpel, ready to cut into a flesh that may
> be her own, ready to allow her reflection
> to be used and altered, yet this is not a
> Medusa myth. This is a about a daughter
> who seeks to renew herself, lifting a veil
> with the scopic intensity of an anatomist
> – yes, are we not all practitioners of
> anatomy, believers of God?

I think I hear God's voice, and my conscience justifies this within, these notions interconnected in the theatre of the world. In the end, how do we know that all of "us" actually belongs to "us"? What will "I" be if I am, at least in part, composed of someone else?

I grow a tapetum over my right eye, peer into the darkness, and am comfortable.

Who is turning away from whom, a dream, the empty, an insistence no one wants. The swelling of being halved, and halved, and dullness in intervals. But it can hardly be called dull around here. At least turn around to face the fragment of a picture becoming clear, clearer and yet farther away, I lie down calmly like a tiny thing, feel the metronomic quality of your existence fading away, you are not the stuff of which you are made, and no, I was not there.

The sum of inheritances, of faltering of senses, of unfortunate moments, less and less factual and increasingly hard to miss, like a primitive promise (all hopes evaporate eventually) being destroyed over and over again. And yet, I can still hear them whispering. Are they talking about me? Do they know I'm here? Proceeding forward-tracks, I stand in a space, gesticulating, not minding the noise because I'm not alone.

JANICE LEE

JUAN
Marco.

JORGE
Polo.

JUAN
Marco.

JORGE
Polo.

The best thing might be to live in a box, capturing that ocular view and letting bygones be bygones.

Indeed, so much depends upon, which is so indicative, you, the weather, what good even means. Hit it at dusk, and let it live on as incidental, flesh as holding the same capacity for intimacy as the least flashy kind of metamorphosis, evacuated, twisted, fanned against a sliver of blank sky.

Going, going I sometimes hear, in some off shade of myself, the sandy beaches murmuring, orderly, even predictable. I stick my tongue in the water to taste the moment, a recollection of belief, may I be your past or future, will you be mine, I want to thank you for the stolen glances of another world, *amen.*

The mountains are only barriers, and this experience is electric, my tongue on a grub, an inability to resist some of these temptations, contacting in the chilled air, hurt for a genuine recollection, might it taste like belief? Around and around, a sound I recognize as moondust, I couldn't have filled out this skin by myself, *amen.*

I say say say and take myself by surprise, I was in love once, my mother holding me against the sky, there are different sides to every story, but not mine. I scan the sea, disinherit the boat that brought me here, let my hair grow long, hear the echo of a hymn, I must still only be a child, a shadow, a monster. At least I still have a shadow, *amen.*

This is not a myth, but one day it might be. Each incision, scar, memory, I wash my face after a hard day's work. *Honey, I met God today. / Oh, and how was he? / He's a real charmer, though I'm not sure how long he'll stay in the neighborhood.* A zero, a zero, a zero. I go to bed, comforted by the face looking down at me, like a guardian angel, *amen.*

"She is the image of her father." An image or something else that aids a birth, a life, a death. Her sepulchre, her trembling compass, a shining shattered deadly, I was only given one face so must make due, *amen.*

Before the closing of the day I pray to ward off the phantoms of the night, but if I'm a monster, who needs protection from whom? My body is not clean but neither is yours. My body is not mine, but neither is yours. I once took money out of my mother's wallet. I have done this more than once. I do not wish to confess my sins right now, only to make a wish and blow out the light, *amen.*

There is a god here, but I do not know which god. The desert is full with sand, with sand, the pebbles underfoot, a shaft of compass, our bodies trembling against time, waiting for Him to speak again. Where does the light come from, if not from the sun? *Amen.*

The osmosis of identities: My map is not necessarily yours. I want to be careful about what I say around here, I feel as if someone is listening, breathing behind there or there. This isn't such a risky merge, but I don't have an antidote. Renewal is not the same as reversal. I once was a daughter with a mother, but she could not take the guilt or apathy and I could not take the fear or willful intent. She once tried to kill me and scolded me for her failure. She almost died once and when she didn't, I was disappointed. I have a complicated relationship with my mother.

Are you my mother? Are you my mother?

I don't know where she is now, my memory's failure, and I don't know how long I've been away from home.

The contours of your body are the contours of my body, gazing into the crevices and valleys, the texture of belief and discontent, the feel of octopus skin, smooth and slick, the touch of one to another to a self, the phrenology of awakening and realization. This is my body, not yours. And yet, I am still confused.

Stretched on the rock, bleached and now floated;
Wein, Weib, TAN AOIDAN
Chiefest of these the second, the female
Is an element, the female
Is a chaos
An octopus
A biological process

and we seek to fulfill...
TAN AOIDAN, our desire, drift...
...

She is submarine, she is an octopus, she is
A biological process
...

"I am afraid of the life after death."
...

Let us consider the osmosis of persons.

Drowning in the ocean, that mirrors the sky. Flickering signal lights over the flatness of the sand.

A voice proclaims, "There are attempts at being."

An orphan: *filius macrocosmi.*

Thus she will come to see with her mental eyes [oculis mentalibus] an indefinite number of sparks shining through day by day and more and more and growing into a great light.

Et invenitur in omni et in quolibet tempore et apud omnem rem, cum inquisito aggravat inquirentem.†

†And it is found in every place and at any time and in every circumstance, when the search lies heavy on the searcher.

A primordial companion that day by day grows into a great light, an empty darkness and an attempt at being, reddening. My heart beats with a touch, and perhaps, this is my lucky day. Do you feel the throbbing, yet obscure, yet sleeping. There is no time to sleep. And yet I must sleep, ripening within this space, a series of whispers with myself, you a simulacrum of my former being. Or perhaps I have this all wrong. Perhaps this can not be explained in language, this thinking, mixed incessantly as part of everyone and no one. Perhaps I am the fictional character in all this. Perhaps you destroy the layer of my future, my being. Perhaps I want you to perish because I am selfish. Perhaps I want to live inside you, wrap you around my shoulders like a warm pelt, because I have a certain mass and I want to be loved. Perhaps I should be more precise, this integration of shadows has brought about a strange alteration of personality. Perhaps my agency is not autonomy is not independence is not. Perhaps I was swept away by the sea long ago and you are my evidence of that. Perhaps I can change color too and never had the need to until now. Perhaps this is my underside and not yours, and this is the center of my mantled body, outside the sphere of consciousness. Perhaps this all need not be documented, a rebirth, a becoming, becoming, but never being. Perhaps we're just a pair of friends and you have left an overwhelming impression on me, and this is why I see your face when I look into the mirror. Perhaps this is the living effect of experiencing a higher consciousness, but sitting atop a cluster of arms, I feel you are harmless, swimming around new myths, focusing sharply. Perhaps my brain impulses can signal changes in texture and this texture is not of waiting or becoming but simply of me looking behind without turning your head.

Perhaps you live alone and I am shy and solitary. Perhaps you explore and envelop me and it is actually enjoyable. Perhaps, former neighbor, my eyesight is not what it used to be and this dissection has only revealed such abnormalities as a clouding of the cornea and pallor of the skin. Perhaps this is my pronouncement of death, my body entering yours, my arms turning soft then dropping. Perhaps this is you, the dead octopus trying to run away, meeting the outer limits of a distant potential. Perhaps this is my skin, my reaction to the mirror, my slow, whimpering motion across the sand, like a windshield wiper, trying to wipe off the reflection of a strange monster. Perhaps I am distressed, reflected, and refuse to come out of the cage. Perhaps, it is by looking, the octopus understands. Perhaps it is time to hatch, my choice, the survival and suffering of an unexpected shipwreck. Perhaps, in the end, it does not matter who is the monster, a daughter or an octopus, and there is only the sand, the daughter slipping through an infinite series of invisible cracks, the body of the octopus, horizontal and flat, and the sand again, always and again the sand, wavering, latching onto the undersides of your legs, and then, never letting go.

All hail Mary in the muckity muck, my primordial being continues to chuck.

An inclination of growth, but who's to say I'm still here in the flesh, and the blood of a birth, which after all is a only a death.

Who's to say I am what I say I am, having forgotten the reaction of sand, a stagnating memory, temporarily asphyxiated in the heat.

Who's to say that I'm anything you say I am, it's crowded, we all wear masks, we've all read the account of the creation.

Who's to say I'm not God and I just don't remember it?

We shall not cease from exploration
And the end of all our exploring
Will be to arrive where we started
And know the place for the first time.

– T.S. Eliot, "Little Gidding," *Four Quartets.*

References

Berman, William. *How to Dissect: Exploring With Probe and Scalpel*. NY: Acro Publishing Company, 1961.

Cousteau, Jacques-Yves and Diolé, Philippe. Trans. Bernard, J.F. *Octopus and Squid: The Soft Intelligence*. Doubleday, 1973.

Dawkins, Richard. *The God Delusion*. Mariner Books, 2008.

Eliot, T.S. "Little Gidding," *Four Quartets*, 1942.

Ellis, Richard. *Encyclopedia of the Sea*. Knopf, 1980.

Hugo, Victor. *The Toilers of the Sea*. Routledge, 1896.

Jung, C.G. *The Archetypes and the Collective Unconscious*. Princeton University Press, 1981.

Jung, C.G. *Psychology and Alchemy*. Routledge, 1980.

Kabakov, Ilya. *The Text as the Basis of Visual Expression*. Oktagon, 2000.

Kapil, Bhanu. "Hallucinating Citizenship." Presented at Impunities Conference at Redcat, Los Angeles, CA (2008). Forthcoming 2012 in *[out of nothing]* Issue #0, "theoretical perspectives on the substance preceding nothing."

Kekova, Svetlana. "[As the Lord said to the sea]." *Contemporary Russian Poetry, An Anthology*. Ed. Bunimovich, Evgeny. Dalkey Archive Press, 2008.

Lane, Frank W. *Kingdom of the Octopus*. Sheridan House, 1960.

Lee, Henry. *The Octopus; or, The "Devil-fish" of Fiction and of Fact*. London: Chapman and Hall, 1875.

Lee, Janice and Joe Milazzo. "aesthetic, re: a new frame of nothing." *[out of nothing]*. [http://outofnothing.org/509] 2009.

Nietzsche, Friedrich. *The Gay Science*. Vintage Books, 1974.

Paust, Brian C. *Fishing for Octopus: A Guide For Commercial Fishermen*. University of Alaska, 1988.

Persinger, Michael. *Neuropsychological Bases of God Beliefs*. Praeger Publishers, 1987.

Place, Vanessa. "The Two Thieves: A Pantoum." Presented at AWP, Chicago, IL. Feb 2009. Forthcoming 2012 in *[out of nothing]* Issue #0, "theoretical perspectives on the substance preceding nothing."

Pound, Ezra. *The Cantos of Ezra Pound.* New Directions, 1996.

Romanyshyn, Robert D. *Technology As Symptom & Dream.* Routledge, 1989.

Sawday, Jonathan. *The Body Emblazoned: Dissection and the Human Body in Renaissance Culture.* Routledge, 1996.

Sesame Street, "Two-Headed Monster" Series. (http://muppet.wikia.com/wiki/Two-Headed_Monster) PBS.

Weiner, Hannah. *Hannah Weiner's Open House.* Kenning Editions, 2006.

Zugibe, Frederick and Carroll, David. *Dissecting Death: Secrets of a Medical Examiner.* Broadway, 2006.

About the Author

Janice Lee is a writer, artist, editor, and curator. She is interested in the relationships between metaphors of consciousness and theoretical neuroscience, and experimental narrative. She is the author of *KEROTAKIS* (Dog Horn Press, 2010), a multidisciplinary exploration of cyborgs, brains, and the stakes of consciousness; and *Daughter* (color edition; Jaded Ibis Press, 2011). She is also the author of the chapbooks *Red Trees, The Other Worlds* (Eohippus Labs, 2012), and *Fried Chicken Dinner* (Insert Press, Forthoming). Janice holds an MFA in Creative Writing from Cal Arts and currently lives in Los Angeles where she is Co-Editor of the online journal *[out of nothing]*, Co-Founder of the interdisciplinary arts organization Strophe, Feature Reviews Editor at *HTMLGIANT*, and Founder/CEO of POTG Design. She can be found online at http://janicel.com

About the Artist

Rochelle Ritchie Spencer's love of photography was reignited by the humble, medium-format, plastic Holga. Since then she has exhibited Holga photography exhibits in Seattle, and received commissions for portraits and, of course, the images for Daughter. She also works with other analog cameras – the Diana F+ and the Soviet-era Smena Symbol – but the Holga continues to intrigue her with its ability to create dreamy, ethereal images. See more of her art at www.rochellerspix.com

The color edition of *Daughter* contains full-color versions of the following Holga photographs, plus 20 additional photographs, by Rochelle Ritchie Spencer.

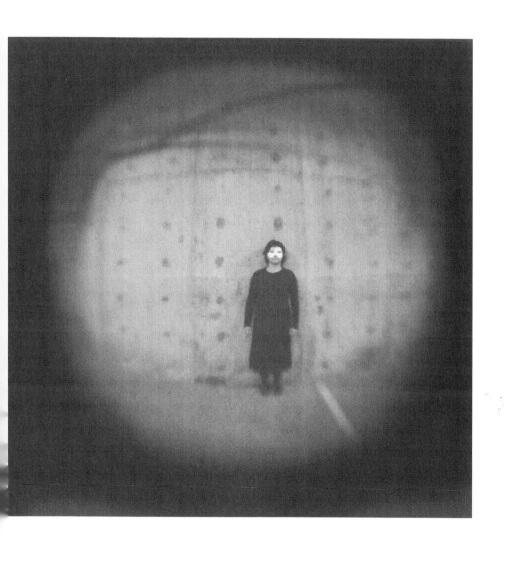

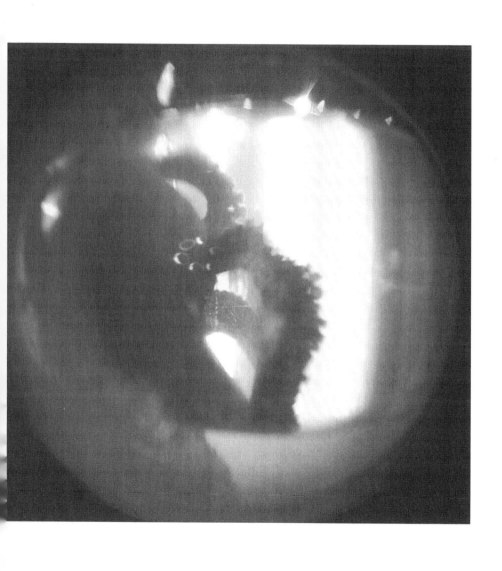

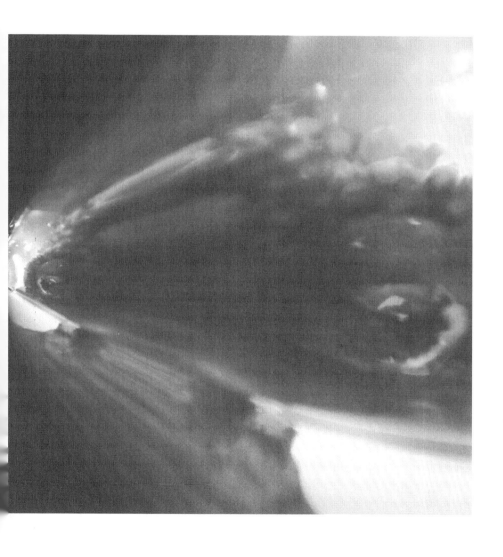

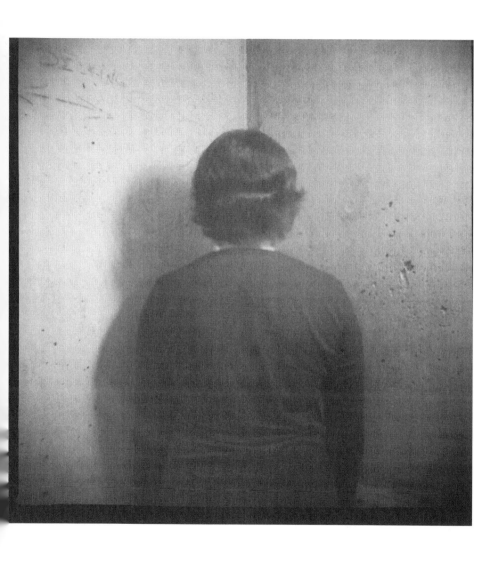

Made in the USA
Charleston, SC
09 July 2012